What Would You Do?

What Would You Do?

by **Pauline Watson**
illustrated by **Sam Q. Weissman**

Prentice-Hall, Inc.
Englewood Cliffs, N.J.

Printed in the United States of America   · J
Prentice-Hall International, Inc., London
Prentice-Hall of Australia, Pty. Ltd., North Sydney
Prentice-Hall of Canada, Ltd., Toronto
Prentice-Hall of India Private Ltd., New Delhi
Prentice-Hall of Japan, Inc., Tokyo
Prentice-Hall of Southeast Asia Pte. Ltd., Singapore
Whitehall Books Limited, Wellington, New Zealand

1 2 3 4 5 6 7 8 9 10
Library of Congress Cataloging in Publication Data
Watson, Pauline.
What would you do?
SUMMARY: Asks a group of youngsters and the reader to decide how
they would handle different situations such as giving away a pet,
starting a new language, or meeting a creature from outer space.
[1. Decision making—Fiction]   I. Weissman, Sam Q.   II. Title.
PZ7.W3285Wh   [E]   79-16296
ISBN 0-13-955252-9

What Would You Do?

What would you do—
If your name was Oh-Oh-Silly-Toe, would you call yourself, Silly-Toe, or just plain Oh-Oh?

What would *you* do?

What would you do—
If you had a dog and a cat and your parents said that you had to give one away?

What would *you* do?

What would you do—
If your friend was always breaking something that belonged to you?

What would *you* do?

What would you do—
If you could whistle louder than a train, one time only, where and when would you whistle?

What would *you* do?

What would you do—
If everything that your right hand touched turned to gold?

What would *you* do?

What would you do—
If you had to make up new words to start a new language, what would you call a baby monkey?

What would *you* do?

What would you do—
If a creature from another planet told you to get into his flying saucer?

What would *you* do?

What would you do—
If a little ghost puppy followed you around and you were the only one who could see it?

What would *you* do?

What would you do—
If you were mistaken for Bad Bump Burney
and you were taken to jail?

What would *you* do?

What would you do—
If you moved to a new town and the only one who wanted to be your friend was a dinosaur with three heads?

What would *you* do?

What would you do—
If a magician turned you into a horse, how would you tell your worried parents that the horse was really you?

What would *you* do?

What would you do—
If a witch landed in your den?

What would *you* do?

What would you do—
If it started to rain ice cream?

What would *you* do?